Room on the Broom

For Natasha, Sabrina and Jasmine – J.D.

First published 2001 by Macmillan Children's Books
This edition published 2002 by Macmillan Children's Books
This book and CD set published 2009 by Macmillan Children's Books
a division of Macmillan Publishers Limited
20 New Wharf Road, London N1 9RR
Basingstoke and Oxford
Associated companies throughout the world
www.panmacmillan.com

ISBN: 978-0-330-50891-9

Text copyright © Julia Donaldson 2001
Illustrations copyright © Axel Scheffler 2001
Interactive e-book CD created by Pat & Pals www.patandpals.com
copyright © Macmillan Children's Books 2009
Moral rights asserted.

3 5 7 9 8 6 4

A CIP catalogue record is available for this book from the British Library.

Printed in Belgium

Room on the Broom

by Julia Donaldson

Illustrated by Axel Scheffler

MACMILLAN
CHILDREN'S BOOKS

The witch had a cat
  and a very tall hat,
And long ginger hair
  which she wore in a plait.
How the cat purred
  and how the witch grinned,
As they sat on their broomstick
  and flew through the wind.

But how the witch wailed
  and how the cat spat,
When the wind blew so wildly
  it blew off the hat.

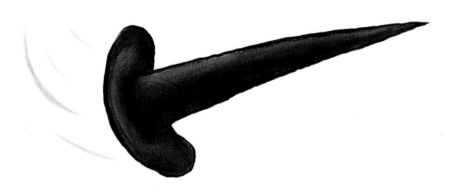

"Down!" cried the witch,
 and they flew to the ground.
They searched for the hat
 but no hat could be found.

Then out of the bushes
 on thundering paws
There bounded a dog
 with the hat in his jaws.

He dropped it politely,
  then eagerly said
(As the witch pulled the hat
  firmly down on her head),
  "I am a dog, as keen as can be.
  Is there room on the broom
  for a dog like me?"

"Yes!" cried the witch,
  and the dog clambered on.
The witch tapped the broomstick and
  whoosh! they were gone.

Over the fields and the
forests they flew.
The dog wagged his tail
and the stormy wind blew.
The witch laughed aloud
and held onto her hat,
But away blew the bow
from her long ginger plait!

Then out from a tree,
    with an ear-splitting shriek,
There flapped a green bird
    with the bow in her beak.
She dropped it politely
    and bent her head low,

"Down!" cried the witch,
    and they flew to the ground.
They searched for the bow
    but no bow could be found.

Then said (as the witch
    tied her plait in a bow),
"I am a bird,
    as green as can be.
Is there room on the broom
    for a bird like me?"

"Yes!" cried the witch,
    so the bird fluttered on.
The witch tapped the broomstick and
    whoosh! they were gone.

Over the reeds and the
rivers they flew.
The bird shrieked with glee
and the stormy wind blew.
They shot through the sky
to the back of beyond.
The witch clutched her bow
but let go of her wand.

"Down!" cried the witch,
and they flew to the ground.
They searched for the wand
but no wand could be found.

Then all of a sudden
        from out of a pond
Leapt a dripping wet frog
        with a dripping wet wand.
He dropped it politely,
        then said with a croak
(As the witch dried the wand
        on a fold of her cloak),
"I am a frog, as clean as can be.
Is there room on the broom
        for a frog like me?"
"Yes!" cried the witch, so the frog
        bounded on.

The witch tapped the broomstick and
        whoosh! they were gone.
Over the moors and the
        mountains they flew.
The frog jumped for joy and . . .

. . . THE BROOM SNAPPED IN TWO!

Down fell the cat and the dog
and the frog.
Down they went tumbling
into a bog.

The witch's half-broomstick
flew into a cloud,
And the witch heard a roar
that was scary and loud . . .

"I am a dragon, as mean as can be,
And I'm planning to have WITCH
        AND CHIPS for my tea!"
"No!" cried the witch,
        flying higher and higher.
The dragon flew after her,
        breathing out fire.
"Help!" cried the witch,
        flying down to the ground.
She looked all around
        but no help could be found.

The dragon drew nearer and,
        licking his lips,
Said, "Maybe this once
        I'll have witch without chips."

But just as he planned
to begin on his feast,
From out of a ditch
rose a horrible beast.
It was tall, dark and sticky,
and feathered and furred.
It had four frightful heads,
it had wings like a bird.
And its terrible voice,
when it started to speak,
Was a yowl and a growl
and a croak and a shriek.
It dripped and it squelched
as it strode from the ditch,
And it said to the dragon,
"Buzz off! –
THAT'S MY WITCH!"

The dragon drew back
and he started to shake.
"I'm sorry!" he spluttered.
"I made a mistake.
It's nice to have met you,
but now I must fly."
And he spread out his wings
and was off through the sky.

Then down flew the bird
and down jumped the frog.
Down climbed the cat,
and "Phew!" said the dog.
And, "Thank you, oh, thank you!"
the grateful witch cried.
"Without you I'd be
in that dragon's inside."

Then she filled up her cauldron
and said with a grin,
"Find something, everyone,
throw something in!"
So the frog found a lily,
the cat found a cone,
The bird found a twig
and the dog found a bone.

They threw them all in
    and the witch stirred them well,
And while she was stirring
    she muttered a spell.
"Iggety, ziggety, zaggety, ZOOM!"

Then out rose . . .

. . . A TRULY MAGNIFICENT BROOM!

With seats for the witch
    and the cat and the dog,
A nest for the bird and
    a shower for the frog.

"Yes!" cried the witch,
    and they all clambered on.
The witch tapped the broomstick and
    whoosh! they were gone.

There are lots more brilliant books by
Julia Donaldson and Axel Scheffler for you to collect:

ISBN: 978-0-333-71093-7

ISBN: 978-0-333-90338-4

ISBN: 978-1-4050-3470-8

ISBN: 978-0-333-98224-2

ISBN: 978-1-4050-2046-6

ISBN: 978-1-407108-82-7

ISBN: 978-0-333-72001-1

ISBN: 978-1-407106-21-2

ISBN: 978-1-4050-0477-0

ISBN: 978-0-333-96396-8

ISBN: 978-0-230-70758-0

ISBN: 978-0-230-70759-7

ISBN: 978-0-230-70859-4

ISBN: 978-0-230-52881-9

ISBN: 978-0-230-53238-0

ISBN: 978-0-230-70860-0

And visit www.gruffalo.com for Gruffalo activities, games and fun!

All Pan Macmillan titles can be ordered from our website, www.panmacmillan.com, or from your local bookshop, and are also available by post from:

Bookpost, PO Box 29, Douglas, Isle of Man IM99 1BQ
Credit cards accepted. For details: Telephone: 01624 677237 Fax: 01624 670923
Email: bookshop@enterprise.net
www.bookpost.co.uk
Free postage and packing in the United Kingdom